Flying Feet

PATRICIA REILLY GIFF

Flying Feet

illustrated by

ALASDAIR BRIGHT

WENDY
LAMB
BOOKS

The author would like to thank Carol Lynn Kearney, senior adjunct in the Department of Communication Sciences and Disorders at Adelphi University, for her careful attention to the manuscript, and advice.

Wendy Lamb Books and the colophon are trademarks of Random House, Inc.

Visit us on the Web! www.randomhouse.com/kids
Educators and librarians, for a variety of teaching tools, visit us at www.randomhouse.com/teachers

Library of Congress Cataloging-in-Publication Data
Giff, Patricia Reilly.
Flying feet / Patricia Reilly Giff ; illustrated by Alasdair Bright. — 1st ed.
p. cm.
Summary: Charlie often thinks of inventions that seldom work, but his latest idea just might be able to help Jake the Sweeper get rid of a big pile of trash and save "Come as a Character" day, too.
ISBN 978-0-385-73887-3 (hc) — ISBN 978-0-385-90754-5 (lib. bdg.) —
ISBN 978-0-375-89637-8 (ebook) — ISBN 978-0-375-85911-3 (pbk.)
[1. Schools—Fiction. 2. Inventors and inventions—Fiction.]
I. Bright, Alasdair, ill. II. Title.
PZ7.G3626Fly 2011
[E]—dc22
2010022645

Printed in the United States of America
10 9 8 7 6 5 4 3 2 1
First Edition

Love to Mari-joy's boys,
Will and Jack O'Leary—P.R.G.

• • •

To my good friend Lucky Jacobs—A.B.

Yolanda

Sumiko

Charlie

Destiny

Gina

Mitchell

Clifton

Trevor

Habib

Beebe

Angel

Peter

CHAPTER 1

FRIDAY

Charlie counted in his head. *Three. Two. One.*

Brrrriiiinnnng!

The three o'clock bell.

It was time for Afternoon Center.

Everyone was going outside today. Some kids were playing basketball. Some kids were doing a potato race.

Charlie had a new invention.

Wait until everyone saw it. They'd be yelling, *"Char-lie, Char-lie!"*

He was even wearing his brother Larry's good luck T-shirt.

Larry was in high school now. He'd gone to the Zigzag School, too. He'd read every book in the library. Even the boring ones.

The teachers still remembered him.

Larry's shirt said WISHBONE on the collar.

Charlie was wishing, all right.

Wishing his invention would work.

Charlie grabbed his bag. "Come on, guys," he yelled. "Invention time."

He raced downstairs and outside. A bunch of kids raced, too.

"Wait up, Charlie," Destiny called. Today she had braids and beads all over her head.

Beebe, a new girl, was with her. Her hair was the color of a carrot.

"I don't hear very well," she told Charlie.

She flipped up her curly hair.

He could see little tan circles in her ears.

"Hearing aids," she said. "They help me hear better."

Charlie leaned against the wall to wait. The school was long and yellow. The bricks were warm.

Beebe was still talking. "My name is Beebe. Like two 'B's."

Charlie nodded. He could see Ramón, the college helper. Ramón was bouncing balls at the handball court.

Sumiko burst out the door. "I'm here." She had a book in her hand. It had a bunch of Japanese words.

Habib came out next. He was juggling two Popsicle sticks. "Me too."

"I hope your invention is good," Mitchell told Charlie.

"Did you ever see anyone walk up a wall?" Charlie asked.

"You're going to do that?" Mitchell asked.

"You'll see." Charlie tapped his bag.

"Hey, Ramón," Mitchell called. "Charlie's going to be a human fly."

Charlie's heart began to pound.

If only this worked.

He'd be a hero.

ZELDA A ZIGZAG

CHARLIE

His picture would be on the wall. Right next to Zelda A. Zigzag's. She had been the first principal of the school.

Charlie opened the bag. He took out his Flying Feet.

He'd been working on the feet for days.

It had started with a buzz in his head.

That was the way all his inventions began.

Buzz! An idea!

He'd taken Larry's thrown-away sneakers. They were huge.

He'd found suction cups on his father's workbench.

He'd glued. . . .

Painted the sneakers bright red. . . .

Outrageous!

Now he took off his socks. His toes had to hold on.

He edged his feet into them. Perfect. Flying Feet!

Ramón frowned. "Are you sure you can do this?"

Charlie wasn't so sure. He had to do it, though.

The whole Afternoon Center was watching.

"Stand back." He made swimming motions with his arms. "I need room."

Mitchell's sister, Angel, shook her head. "We're going to need an ambulance," she told Ramón.

"I'm right here," Ramón said. "Don't worry."

Charlie wanted to tell Angel to be quiet. But she remembered his last invention.

The Breathe-Underwater Box.

He'd nearly drowned.

Charlie wiggled his toes in the Flying Feet.

Larry's sneakers were a lot bigger than his feet.

He hoped they'd stay on.

"Go, go, go, go," Mitchell and Habib yelled.

"Stop, stop," Angel said.

Charlie took a look at the handball wall.

He took five steps back. Then he began to run.

He could see Angel. Her hands covered her eyes.

The wall was in front of him.

He took a giant step. Up. The sneaker stuck to the wall.

It was going to work!

Charlie, the greatest inventor in the Center.

His foot slipped out of the sneaker.

"Bonk!" he heard Mitchell yell.

Charlie hit the ground.

"I knew it," Angel said. "Call the ambulance."

Ramón helped him up. "He's all right. I have him."

What Charlie had was ten sore toes.

Larry's WISHBONE shirt was ripped.

Worse than all that, his invention had failed.

Again!

CHAPTER 2

MONDAY

Charlie looked under his desk at his feet. His mother had cut out the front of his sneakers.

Band-Aids were stuck on his toes.

Too bad he couldn't invent an Instant Stop-Scratches Pill.

WHAM!

Outside there was an explosion of noise.

"A UFO has crashed!" someone screeched.

"Nonsense," said Ms. Katz.

Charlie stood up. He could see Jake the Sweeper's truck. A huge pile of stuff had fallen off the back.

Jake jumped up and down. He pulled at his hair.

The end-of-the-day bell rang.

Some kids headed for home. But almost everyone headed for the stairs. They were going to the Afternoon Center.

There'd be snack, and climbing in the gym, and a bunch of other things to do.

Charlie limped down the hall as fast as he could. He had to get outside.

He wanted to see what had happened to Jake's truck.

Sumiko walked next to him.

Her ponytail bounced. Her sneakers slapped on the floor.

She had great feet for running, Charlie thought.

"Your invention was a good try," she said.

Charlie swallowed.

His brother, Larry, didn't think it was a good try. Charlie had to give Larry his allowance. Maybe for the rest of his life.

It was because of Larry's ripped WISHBONE shirt.

Someone clapped.

It was Mrs. Farelli, the art teacher.

She was tough. Almost as tough as Zelda A. Zigzag, the school's first principal.

Was she calling him?

"Charles," she shouted. "And Sumiko."

Charlie looked at the door.

He was almost there.

Lucky Sumiko. She dashed outside.

Mrs. Farelli clapped her hands. "I've been looking for someone from the Afternoon Center," she said. "Anyone."

Charlie took turtle steps to the Art Room.

"I have a great idea," Mrs. Farelli said. "Your brother, Larry, would have loved this. Too bad he's not here anymore."

Charlie looked up at her.

He was getting a little sick of Larry.

Mrs. Farelli rushed on. "We're going to have a Come as a Character Day," she said.

The hall was empty. Everyone must be scarfing up cheese poppers in the lunchroom.

"Isn't that grand, Charles?"

Charlie could see Sumiko's ponytail around the edge of the door.

She was hiding at the end of the hall.

She had come back to wait for him.

"We'll dress as book characters," Mrs. Farelli said. "We'll tell everyone a tiny part of each story."

Mrs. Farelli drew herself up. She squinched one eye shut. "Yo-ho-ho. I'm a pirate from *Treasure Island*," she boomed. "And this is how my story begins. . . ."

She unsquinched her eye. "Know what I mean?"

Charlie gulped.

"It'll be a blast," Mrs. Farelli said. "We'll invite the parents to come next Monday. And Mr.

Randolph, the principal, of course. And maybe Zelda Zigzag."

She tapped his arm. "You could ask your brother, Larry. He loves to read."

Larry again! "I don't think—"

Mrs. Farelli tilted her head. "You might even be Peter Rabbit."

Charlie could see himself with long paper ears. He'd have a round cotton tail.

Larry would be laughing his sides out.

What could be more horrible?

"Get all your friends," she said. "Meet me in the art room tomorrow afternoon."

He gave a half nod.

"We do things together at the Zelda A. Zigzag School," she said.

Charlie limped out of the art room.

Sumiko was right outside the door.

Charlie hopped down the hall on one foot. The one with three Band-Aids. His toes hurt.

Sumiko began to laugh. "You really look like Peter Rabbit!" she said.

"I think I need a snack," Charlie said.

They headed for the lunchroom.

CHAPTER 3

STILL MONDAY

Outside, Charlie looked back at the yellow brick school.

He could see Habib across the yard. He was juggling two golf balls. Almost juggling.

They kept rolling away from him.

Mitchell was watching, laughing.

Charlie stopped. "Hey, guys."

"It's Charlie Flying Feet," said Habib.

"I don't want to think about that," Charlie said.

"Think about cheese poppers." Mitchell handed one to him and one to Sumiko. "I've had a ton already."

"Thanks." Charlie put his popper in his mouth. Cheese melted into a bread ball. Mmm.

"Mrs. Farelli grabbed me," he said when he could talk. "She wants—"

"Mrs. Farelli is tough as nails," Mitchell said.

"Almost as tough as Zelda A. Zigzag," said Habib.

"She's going to have a Come as a Character Day." Charlie talked as fast as he could. "Next Monday."

"Sorry," Habib said. "I'm working on juggling."

Mitchell wasn't paying attention. He sprinkled cheese-popper crumbs on the cement. "It's a lunchroom line for ants," he said.

Sumiko leaned over to watch. But Charlie kept going. He hobbled toward Jake.

Destiny stood on the stone wall with Beebe.

Fifth graders were climbing over Jake's pile of stuff.

So was Terrible Thomas, Jake's cat. Oops. Terrible Thomas was Mrs. Thomas now. She'd had a bunch of kittens.

"Out of here!" Jake yelled at everyone. Jake was a yeller.

They all scattered. . . .

Except Mrs. Thomas and Charlie.

"Look at this, Charlie," Jake said. "It's all good stuff. Old but clean. There's just no room for it."

Charlie walked around the pile.

There were lumps of straw and pots of droopy flowers. A tin hat and eyeglasses without the glass. Curtains. Yellow bricks from when the school was built.

The bricks must be as old as Zelda A. Zigzag.

On top were the red Flying Feet.

"I was taking all this to the dump," Jake said. "Then, *BAAAAM*. Two flat tires."

Charlie sat on a falling-apart chair. It was almost an invention. A Three-Legged Tilting Seat.

He looked over at a broken door and a couple of pipes.

"I've got to get rid of this junk," Jake said. "Mr. Randolph, the principal, will have a fit."

"We could drag—"

"Drag it where?" Jake moaned. "I'll never get my work done. The whole school is a mess. Cheese poppers all over the place!"

"We could put it all back on the truck."

Jake sighed. "That's a big job. It took me days to get it out of the storeroom."

"Time for kickball," Ramón yelled.

Charlie jumped off the chair. It kept rocking.

"I'll help you tomorrow," Charlie said. He ran over to the game.

"Charlie's on our side," Habib yelled.

• • •

Afternoon Center was over for today.

Charlie headed for the bus.

He nodded at Mrs. Dover, the bus driver.

Her baseball hat was perched up on her hair.

He went to the back. The whole school didn't have to know that the new bus driver was his mother.

Sumiko sat next to him. Her face was red. "I've been running like a cheetah," she said.

Sumiko was the smartest girl he knew.

She knew sixteen words in Japanese.

Whoosh! The bus started up.

"How about signing up for Come as a Character Day?" Charlie asked Sumiko.

"What?"

"You dress up as someone in a book." He raised his shoulders. "You talk about—"

Sumiko shook her head. "Sorry. I'm training for the Olympics. Ramón says I'm a really fast runner."

Destiny and Beebe sat in front of them.

Destiny patted a sparkly scarf on her head. "My hair isn't so hot today. The beads keep falling out."

"Mrs. Farelli said—" Charlie began.

"Make sure you look at Beebe when you talk," Destiny said. "She can read your lips."

"That's really good," Charlie said.

Beebe grinned. "Yup," she said.

"About Mrs. Farelli," Charlie said.

Destiny stopped patting her hair. "Mrs. Farelli is too tough for me."

"It's for next Monday," he said. "We're going to do Come as a Character Day."

"I'm too busy. I'm going to be a ballroom dancer," Beebe said.

Gina was sitting in front of them. "I'm too

busy, too. I'm going to be an opera star." She opened her mouth. *"Tor-eeeeee-a-dora,"* she sang.

Gina was loud. Screechy.

"Stick to inventing. Don't bother with"— Destiny waved her hand—"come as a . . . whatever."

Charlie looked out the bus window. Next Monday was going to be the worst!

Just Mrs. Farelli and a bunch of parents.

And Charlie, by himself, as Peter Rabbit.

CHAPTER 4

TUESDAY

It was time for Afternoon Center.

Charlie was hiding in the mop closet.

Never mind that the mop was dripping.

Never mind that his shirt was sopping wet.

He could hear kids going down the hall.

Today there was knitting. Some kids were making scarves. Beebe was showing them how.

There was painting, too. Some kids were making flags for the walls.

But Charlie had to think.

The only two who wanted to come as characters were Trevor and Clifton.

Kindergarten kids!

Outside the door, he heard a meow.

It was Mrs. Thomas.

Sometimes she sneaked into school with her six kittens. Sometimes she came alone.

She thought she owned the mop closet.

Charlie opened the door a crack.

Mrs. Thomas darted in. She gave Charlie a quick scratch with one claw.

Yeow. Charlie moved over to give her room.

He peered out the door.

Sumiko was peering in. "What are you doing in there, Charlie?"

He opened the door a little wider.

He wanted to see Sumiko's whole face. Not half a ponytail.

Sumiko leaned closer. "Are you going to stay in there all afternoon?"

Charlie thought about staying in the mop closet.

He could invent something new. Maybe a machine that made dollar bills. He'd be rich.

Too bad it was against the law to make your own money.

Or how about a potato chopper?

Yes! He felt that buzz in his head.

An invention buzz!

He'd stick in a potato.

Out would come French fries. Or potato chips.

What an invention! He'd call it Pop Out a Potato.

Maybe his greatest one yet.

Charlie heard a clack-clack noise. Someone was coming.

"Uh-oh," Sumiko said. "It's Mrs. Farelli."

Charlie leaned back into the mop.

"Did Charles tell you about Come as a Character Day?" Mrs. Farelli asked Sumiko.

"Um."

"Good," Mrs. Farelli said. "I'll see you all in the art room in five minutes."

All, Charlie thought. *All?*

Mrs. Farelli clacked away.

Sumiko slid into the closet. "No Olympics for me," she said.

She gave Charlie a box of raisins. "It's today's snack."

"Thanks." Charlie tore open the box.

They sat there and chewed.

"Not much room in here," Charlie said.

Mrs. Thomas must have thought so, too.

She gave Sumiko a quick scratch. She spit at Charlie.

They dived out of the closet.

Mrs. Farelli was standing at the end of the hall. "There you are," she said.

They followed her into the art room.

"We have so much to do," Mrs. Farelli said. "We have to make costumes and practice."

She rooted through a box. "Nothing in here but . . ."

She held up a feather. She stuck it in her hair. She twirled around.

Mrs. Farelli looked a little like a rooster.

She was smiling. A big rooster smile.

Mrs. Farelli smiling?

Charlie could hardly believe it.

"I don't know what this feather is good for." She leaned over the box. "But look at this."

She held up a fake carrot. "Perfect for our boy Peter Rabbit," she said.

Charlie swallowed.

She dug a little deeper. "Where did these come from?" She held up a pair of fuzzy white pajamas. "An old costume, I guess. Perfect for a rabbit."

Charlie took a step back.

Mrs. Farelli was still smiling. "Are you ready for more news?"

Trevor and Clifton, the kindergarten kids, popped in the door.

"We're ready," Clifton said. "Maybe I'll be Jack the Giant Killer."

"Something tough, anyway." Trevor clenched his fists. "Graaaaaahhhh!"

Charlie jumped. So did Sumiko.

Mrs. Farelli tapped Charlie on the arm. "I saw your brother, Larry. He was outside the high school. I stopped the car and invited him," she said. "He was thrilled."

"I can't believe it," Charlie said.

"Grand, right? I called Zelda A. Zigzag. She'll be coming, too."

Charlie swallowed.

Zelda A. Zigzag and Larry would see him.

He'd be wearing fuzzy white pajamas. They'd watch him chomping down on a fake carrot.

CHAPTER 5

WEDNESDAY

Everyone was going up to the library.

Almost everyone. Beebe and Destiny were knitting in the art room. The scarves looked like skinny red strings.

Mitchell waved at Charlie. "I'm staying for Homework Help. I'm writing the story of my life."

Charlie nodded. Mitchell was the best writer in the Center. He'd won a prize for it.

"We don't even have to think about Come as a Character Day until tomorrow," Charlie told Sumiko.

"Whew," she said.

Behind them, Trevor yelled, "Graaaah!"

No one jumped. It was the tenth time he'd graaaaahed in the last two minutes.

Clifton threw himself on the floor, laughing. "Great growl," he told Trevor.

A sign was taped outside of the library. CLOSE THE DOOR QUICKLY.

Ms. Katz had brought her new dog, Tree Stump, with her.

He was little and round. Just like a tree stump.

Mrs. Thomas, the cat, would eat him ears to tail in one gulp.

Charlie opened the library door a couple of inches. He and Sumiko slipped through.

Tree Stump was safe.

Charlie liked being at the library. Especially during Afternoon Center.

Ms. Katz was the best teacher in school. She wore blue glasses. Her hair was straight as a stick.

It was read-aloud time. Everyone sat on the floor around Ms. Katz. Beebe sat closest. She could read Ms. Katz's lips. Wow!

Ms. Katz passed out carrot cupcakes. They had swirls of icing on top like orange hats.

No one had to worry about crumbs on the rug.

Tree Stump loved crumbs.

Ms. Katz read to them . . .

. . . with all the sound effects.

Last month she had read about a girl named Mary. Mary had found a secret garden.

This month she was reading about Dorothy and a wizard.

Dorothy and her dog, Toto, had been twirled away in a twister, or a rainstorm. One of those things, anyway.

"Swishhhhh, crackle, boooom," Ms. Katz thundered.

"Kiken." Sumiko's eyes were wide. "That's 'danger' in Japanese."

"Graaaaaahhhh!" roared Trevor.

Clifton tried a roar, too. It sounded more like a squeak.

But Tree Stump dived under the table.

Charlie listened. Dorothy had met three guys on the Yellow Brick Road. They all wanted something. They needed a wizard to help.

Charlie heard a noise in back of him.

Habib was juggling with cupcakes.

Splat!

What a mess.

Charlie scooped up icing from the table leg.

Delicious.

Tree Stump scarfed up a chunk from the rug.

He probably thought it was delicious, too.

Ms. Katz read more. She told them that Dorothy wanted to go home. It was lucky she had red shoes. She tapped them together three times. Then she was home.

Charlie liked being home, too.

He had started a new invention in his room.

He'd felt that buzz in his head. It was like a bee buzzing around in there. A thinking bee.

The invention was a Junker Cruncher.

It was a machine to crunch up junk.

If only it would work!

It would help Jake.

It would help the whole world.

All Charlie needed was a motor. And a cruncher. A big cruncher.

So far he had a mousetrap from the garage.

Snap!

It had cut a pen in half.

He'd get the small cruncher going. Then he and Jake could build a gigantic one.

Out in the hall, Ramón blew his whistle. Time to go.

Charlie and Sumiko walked to the bus.

The bus driver was waiting for them. She had a bandage on her foot.

"What happened?" Charlie asked.

Mrs. Dover didn't look happy.

"Snap! I stepped on a mousetrap." She looked at Charlie. "It was in my son's bedroom."

Terrible news! Her poor foot.

And almost as bad—

His Junker Cruncher was ruined.

CHAPTER 6

THURSDAY

This afternoon it was about to rain. Charlie could hear thunder.

"Swish crackle boom," he said to himself in a Ms. Katz voice.

He went downstairs to the Center.

"How about knitting with us?" Destiny asked.

Beebe was standing next to her. "I'll teach you." Beebe sounded just a little loud. Ms. Katz said that was because she couldn't hear her own voice very well.

"You could make a tie," Beebe said.

Beebe was a nice girl. But a tie? He wouldn't wear a tie in a million years. "Sorry," he said.

He looked out the door.

The pile of junk was still there. Jake was trying to cover it.

He flapped a big gray tarp.

Charlie wanted to help. But Mrs. Farelli would be waiting. Charlie walked to the art room. Slowly.

The door was locked.

Ms. Katz came along. "Mrs.  Farelli has a cold," she said. "She'll be out for the rest of the week."

"Too bad," Charlie said.

Wait. Did that mean— No Peter Rabbit!

He raced down the hall. He jumped up. How close could he get to the lights?

Not very close.

He and Sumiko went outside.

On top of the junk pile was an old mirror. Charlie could see Mrs. Thomas in it.

She was taking a nap under the three-legged tilting chair.

Charlie and Sumiko helped Jake flap the tarp over the pile. Fourteen flaps!

The tarp sailed over the three of them: Charlie, Jake, and Sumiko.

"Mr. Randolph wants a clean schoolyard by Monday," Jake said. "Something special is going on."

"Not anymore," Charlie said.

"Special or not," Jake said. "Mr. Randolph said that the pile goes."

Charlie squinted at the pile. "We could dig a hole. Bury the whole thing."

"It would have to be huge. The size of China." Jake closed his eyes. "I'd have to work on Saturday."

"Muda," Sumiko said. "That's 'no good' in Japanese."

"How about a zoo?" Charlie said. He picked up a metal bar. "We could use these."

"Ii," Sumiko said. "That's 'good.'"

Was that a buzz in Charlie's head?

"We could start with Mrs. Thomas and Tree Stump," Charlie said. "We could add a monkey."

He thought about it. "Maybe we could get the real zoo to lend us an ele—"

"Mr. Randolph would fire me," Jake said.

No buzz after all, Charlie thought.

"Time to sweep the halls," Jake said.

It started to rain.

"Time for a snack," Charlie said.

In the lunchroom no one was eating.

No wonder.

The snack was soup.

It was the red kind, with lumps.

"It'll warm you up on this rainy day," the lunch lady said.

Destiny and Beebe were helping the lunch lady. "Get your soup crackers here!" they yelled.

Sumiko backed away. "I might be allergic to soup."

"I'm allergic to lumps," Mitchell said.

"Me too," said Habib.

A couple of kids grabbed crackers. Then they slid out the door.

The lunch lady looked disappointed.

How could Charlie hurt her feelings?

He tried a sip. He kept his teeth closed.

It was the worst.

"Hi, everyone." Ms. Katz was at the lunch-room door.

"How about some soup?" the lunch lady asked her.

"No, thanks," Ms. Katz said. "It's the red kind with lumps."

The lunch lady nodded. "I don't like it, either. But Charlie loves it."

She filled Charlie's bowl again.

Charlie began to shake his head.

"Don't worry," the lunch lady said. "I have tons of it. I'll freeze the rest."

Charlie took half a lump.

It would take a hundred spoonfuls to get to the bottom of the bowl.

Ms. Katz sat down at the table. "Poor Mrs. Farelli," she said to everyone. "She was excited about Come as a Character Day on Monday."

Charlie and Sumiko looked at each other.

"Too bad," Habib said.

"She invited Zelda A. Zigzag. And the parents. And Charlie's older brother, Larry. He's read a million books." Ms. Katz poked at her glasses. "He's a great boy."

"Great. Like red soup with lumps," Charlie said.

"Told you," the lunch lady said. "Charlie loves this soup."

Ms. Katz shook her head. "We have to call off Come as a Character Day. "There's no time to make costumes. No time to practice."

She pushed her glasses up on her hair. "Too bad. Mrs. Farelli always says we do things together at the Zelda A. Zigzag School."

Charlie made himself eat another lump.

"Some ideas are good," Sumiko said. "Some are not so good. That's what my mother says."

Charlie's mother had said that just last night.

He'd been working on his Pop Out a Potato invention.

He'd left a bag of potatoes in the yard.

In the rain.

By accident.

The potatoes had turned to mush.

His mother's potato pancakes had no potatoes.

They were as horrible as the soup.

Charlie knew how Mrs. Farelli must feel.

"Poor tough-as-nails Mrs. Farelli," Sumiko
whispered to Charlie.

"We should have helped her," Habib said.

"Yes," Charlie said.

He pushed his bowl away.

He couldn't eat any more.

CHAPTER 7

STILL THURSDAY

The rain stopped.

A pale sun came out. Everyone ran for the yard.

Ramón blew his whistle. "Who's ready for a race?" he called.

"A race!" Destiny told Beebe.

"Me!" Beebe yelled.

"Me too," Sumiko said.

Charlie watched Sumiko run in place. She was warming up.

A bunch of kids sloshed through the puddles.

Charlie sat on the wall.

The stones were wet.

So what? They felt good.

Trevor and Clifton hopped along the wall. "Great hoppers, right?" Trevor yelled.

"You'd make great Peter Rabbits," Charlie said.

Clifton stopped hopping. He wiggled his nose.

Habib juggled an old ball. "I found it in Jake's junk pile," Habib told Charlie.

"I found this, too." Mitchell waved a horn. "It doesn't toot. I might take it home anyway."

Ramón stood at the other end of the field. He raised his arms high.

Then he snapped them down.

Everyone began to run.

Beebe was running hard. She passed Sumiko.

Her face was red.

She was beating some of the fifth graders.

Clifton jumped off the wall. He just missed Beebe.

"Yeow!" Beebe yelled.

Clifton landed on a box in Jake's pile.

"They're work gloves." Clifton held up a green one.

Charlie felt a buzz.

It was a little buzz.

Still—

Another invention?

He had no time to think about it.

Ms. Katz sat down next to him. "The wall is a little damp," she said. "But it feels good."

Beebe passed him for the second time.

Habib came flying by.

Trevor threw a glove in the air.

Big gloves.

Thick gloves.

Gloves with lots of room.

The buzz in Charlie's head began again.

Jake came along. "Go, guys," he yelled.

"Can I have those gloves?" Charlie asked Jake.

Jake waved his hand. "Take anything. Take it all."

"I feel terrible," Ms. Katz said.

Charlie looked over at her.

She didn't look sick.

She shook her head. "I'm thinking of Mrs. Farelli. She was sad about Monday."

Charlie thought about Mrs. Farelli.

He thought about the feather in her hair.

She had twirled around, singing *tra-la-la*.

She'd looked happy.

"I hate to call Zelda A. Zigzag tomorrow," Ms. Katz said. "She'll be sad, too."

Ramón held up his finger. "Sumiko came in first."

He held up two fingers so Beebe could see. "Beebe second."

"Whew." Sumiko leaned close so Beebe could read her lips. "My feet are falling off."

Charlie felt that buzz again. Louder now.

An invention was on its way, Charlie thought.

Ramón blasted his whistle two times.

The buses were there.

Mrs. Dover, the bus driver, honked her horn.

Charlie grabbed the box of gloves.

He began to run to the bus.

So did some of the other kids.

"What's that box for?" Mrs. Dover asked.

"I don't know yet," he said.

"I hope it isn't Flying Feet," she said. "I hope it doesn't have a mousetrap."

Charlie ducked his head.

"Or an Underwater-Breathing Box."

Charlie went to the back of the bus.

Sumiko slid in next to him. "The bus driver knows a lot about you," she said.

"She's pretty smart," Charlie said.

Sumiko wiggled her legs around. "My feet need a rest," she said.

Charlie nodded.

He wasn't thinking about her feet, though.

He was thinking about a new invention.

He was thinking about poor Mrs. Farelli, too.

CHAPTER 8

FRIDAY

It was early on Friday morning.

Too early for school.

No one would be in the classroom except Ms. Katz.

That was good. That was great.

At home, Charlie zigzagged down the driveway.

He carried the box with his new invention.

"Hurry." He jumped up and down at the bus door.

He and his mother climbed in.

They zoomed over to school.

Charlie left the box on Jake's junk pile.

No one would see it there.

His mother gave a quick honk. She was off to pick up the busers.

Mattheus, the guard, was at the door. "You're early today, Charlie," he said. "March yourself right in."

Charlie could hear the band practicing. *Boom de boom.*

Mrs. Thomas was taking a walk.

Charlie circled around her.

In the principal's office, the light was on.

Charlie could see Mr. Randolph's bald head.

Maybe Mr. Randolph never went home. Maybe he had a bed in his closet.

Charlie was glad he was going to be an inventor.

He wouldn't want to live in the Zelda A. Zigzag School for the rest of his life. At night. In the dark.

He kept going.

Up the stairs.

Down to room 214.

Ms. Katz was working at her desk.

She poked at her glasses. She pushed back her stick-straight hair. "Hey, Charlie," she said.

He wiggled his toes. All the Band-Aids were off now.

"I have a new invention," he said.

"Lovely," Ms. Katz said. It was her favorite word.

"It made me think—"

Ms. Katz stood up. "Thinking is good."

"Could we still have Come as a Character Day?" he asked.

Ms. Katz blinked.

Charlie took a breath. "We could get rid of Jake's junk pile, too."

"That pile out there?" Ms. Katz's eyebrows went up almost to her hair. "And what about characters?"

She leaned forward. "It's Friday, Charlie. Come as a Character Day was supposed to be Monday."

Charlie heard the bus outside. His mother was back with the busers.

The walkers were here, too.

Doors banged.

Feet slapped.

The bell rang.

Gina came down the hall. *"Mama mia, pizza-rii-a,"* she sang.

Whew! She was loud.

Ms. Katz covered her ears. So did Charlie.

Gina passed the door.

Charlie knew she stopped at the water fountain. It sounded as if she might be gargling.

"Well, the Center is open on Saturday." Ms. Katz smiled. "We could work on it tomorrow morning."

She held up her hands. All her fingers were crossed. "We'll give it a try."

Charlie went to his desk. He put his books in a row.

He had a feeling.

Too bad it wasn't a buzz.

He thought about his Flying Feet and his Junker Cruncher.

And what about last year's invention? The Snowball Saver.

Not one of them had worked.

Maybe this new invention wouldn't work, either.

He hoped it would.

Otherwise, everyone would be laughing.

Especially Larry.

CHAPTER 9

SATURDAY

On Saturday morning, Charlie looked around. Almost everyone was at the Center today.

"I had to come," Sumiko said. "I felt sorry for Mrs. Farelli."

Gina nodded. "Me too. Even though she's tough as nails."

"Besides," Habib said, "the lunch lady has a great snack today."

It was Charlie's favorite.

Destiny and Beebe were giving them out. Fat pretzels with white salt dots on top.

Charlie chewed on the white pretzel dots.

Then he went with Mitchell to the Homework Help room. But there wasn't any Homework Help on Saturday.

Today it was just a regular classroom.

Mitchell pulled out a paper and pen. "What should I write?"

"Write a story to go with my new invention," Charlie said.

Mitchell stared up at the ceiling. "What's it called?"

Charlie stared out the window. What was it called?

Nothing yet.

"Wizard Walkers," he said, after a minute.

Charlie looked at the stone wall outside. Jake was taking off the tarp.

He'd show everyone his invention there.

He looked over Mitchell's shoulder. "Nothing is on your paper," he said. "It's just a big blank."

"Listen, Charlie," Mitchell said. "I have to think first."

"Start with the title," Charlie said.

"Why don't you go outside?" Mitchell said. "Help everyone with Jake's pile. You can watch everyone practice."

"I hope you know how to spell 'wizard,'" Charlie said.

"Of course," Mitchell said. "'W-i-s-s-e-r-d.'"

"Good."

Outside, Destiny ran past him.

She was carrying a watering can from Jake's pile.

It was full of water now.

It sloshed across the schoolyard.

"Out of my way, Charlie," Destiny said. "I have to water those half-dead plants in the junk pile. I'm going to save their lives."

Charlie followed her across the yard. He found the box with his invention.

He found a penny, too. A penny for luck!

Ms. Katz rocked back and forth on the three-legged tilting chair. Her hair was flying around.

Everyone dug through the junk pile.

They were looking for things to go with their characters.

Angel opened a box. "Here's a blue ribbon for my hair," she said. "I guess I'll be Alice in Wonderland."

Gina tossed Charlie's red Flying Feet sneakers out of the way. "They're really junk," she said.

Sumiko scooped them up.

She held them in the air.

She squinted at them.

"Not junk at all," she said. "I know what to do with them."

"All this straw." Jake scratched his head. "I don't know where it came from."

"Never mind," Habib said. "I know what to do with it."

He dragged some of it away.

Charlie stood there with his hands on his hips.

Jake's junk pile was smaller.
The stone wall looked bigger.
Never mind, Charlie told himself.
He was going to be brave.
He had to do it.

CHAPTER 10

MONDAY

The bell rang.

It was Come as a Character Day.

There was no time for snack.

But who wanted snack anyway?

The lunch lady had warmed a huge pot of red soup with lumps.

Outside, everything was ready.

Jake had used the bricks to make a yellow

brick road. It went straight to the stone wall.

He'd put a bunch of chairs out, too.

Destiny and Sumiko stood behind the pile. They were getting ready.

Habib and Mitchell were getting ready, too.

Charlie held the paper Mitchell had written.

His invention box was right in front of him.

He was ready. Maybe.

Mr. Randolph, the principal, came across the yard. Mrs. Farelli was next to him.

Her nose was red, but she was smiling.

People were at the gate, too.

"Wow," said Mitchell. "There's Zelda A. Zigzag. She looks just like her picture."

Charlie looked up.

Larry walked with Zelda A. Zigzag. He helped her to her seat. A special seat Jake had brought from the office.

But she pointed to the three- legged tilting

chair. "I'll sit there," she said. "I like adventure."

"Hey," Sumiko said. "Even the bus driver came."

All the seats were taken.

Beebe gave out programs. "I made them last night," she said.

Ms. Katz stood up. "Come as a Character Day is in honor of Mrs. Farelli. We're glad she's back."

Charlie blinked. It was true. He *was* glad.

Everyone clapped.

"Now we'll begin," said Ms. Katz.

Trevor Petway hopped out from behind the pile. His friend Clifton hopped, too. They wore paper rabbit ears.

"Graaaaahhhh!" they shouted. "We're Peter Rabbits. Tough ones."

Gina came out next. Her hair was slicked back. A curtain hung from her shoulders. She wore the ruined eyeglasses from the pile.

"Do you know who I am?" she asked.

"Everyone knows that," Zelda A. Zigzag said.

"You're Harry Potter. And we know your story."

Mitchell wore a tin hat.

Habib had straw sticking out of his sleeves.

"We're characters from Dorothy's story," they said together.

Sumiko popped out behind them. She held Ms. Katz's dog, Tree Stump.

She wore the red Flying Feet sneakers.

She tapped them together three times. "See? Ruby-red sneakers."

She looked around. "There's no place like home," she said. "Oops, I forgot to say I'm Dorothy. This is my dog, Toto."

Sumiko stopped. "These are also Flying Feet. I'll touch them for luck for the next race."

Tree Stump jumped out of her arms. Beebe chased him. "Got him!" she said.

Charlie heard voices behind him.

"This is great," Zelda A. Zigzag was whispering to Mrs. Farelli.

Would his part be great? Charlie wondered. Or would Larry laugh?

Destiny came next. She had yellow streaks in her hair. "I'm Mary. Some people might think this is a pile of junk."

She waved her arms around. "But it's a secret garden. See the flowers? See the pipes that make a little fence around them?"

"Good ideas," said Mr. Randolph.

"Wow," Jake said.

Then it was Charlie's turn.

He went to the box.

Inside were the work gloves.

They looked huge.

They were stuffed with cotton.

There was just room for his hands.

But first he read Mitchell's paper. "This is the story of an inventor named Charlie," he said. "He invented Wizard Walkers."

"Who ever heard of that story?" Gina asked.

"It's a new one," Charlie said. "It was written by Mitchell McCabe."

Mitchell took a bow.

"Lovely," said Ms. Katz.

Charlie snapped on the gloves. He waved them in the air. "These are Wizard Walkers. Dorothy's wizard might have used them."

"Lovely," said Sumiko in a Ms. Katz voice.

Charlie climbed up on the wall.

He crouched down.

He leaned on his hands.

He threw his legs up in the air.

And began to walk on his hands.

One hand-step.

Two.

He was going to fall. "Yeow . . ."

But then someone held on to his ankles.

"Everyone needs a helper," a voice said. "Even a wizard."

It was Larry. He wasn't laughing.

Charlie kept going along the wall. Right to the end.

He still owed Larry T-shirt money. He'd give him the penny he'd found. That was a good start.

Then he stood up. "I have more Wizard Walkers in the box," he said. "Help yourself."

Mrs. Farelli nodded. "We all do things together at the Zelda A. Zigzag School. We do them for each other."

Everyone was clapping.

"Time for snack," Mrs. Farelli said. "Red soup."

Zelda A. Zigzag was twirling on the

three-legged twirling chair. She stood up. "Ah.
The wonderful red kind with lumps."

Charlie walked with her.

He might try a little more of that soup, too.

He felt a buzz. Was it about soup?

A new invention was on the way.

He just had to figure out how to do it.

Buzzzzz.

PATRICIA REILLY GIFF is the author of many beloved books for children, including the Kids of the Polk Street School books, the Friends and Amigos books, and the Polka Dot Private Eye books. Several of her novels for older readers have been chosen as ALA-ALSC Notable Books and ALA-YALSA Best Books for Young Adults. They include *The Gift of the Pirate Queen; All the Way Home; Water Street; Nory Ryan's Song,* a Society of Children's Book Writers and Illustrators Golden Kite Honor Book for Fiction; and the Newbery Honor Books *Lily's Crossing* and *Pictures of Hollis Woods. Lily's Crossing* was also chosen as a *Boston Globe–Horn Book* Honor Book. Her most recent books are *Number One Kid, Eleven, Wild Girl,* and *Storyteller.* Patricia Reilly Giff lives in Connecticut.

ALASDAIR BRIGHT is a freelance illustrator who has worked on numerous books and advertising projects. He loves drawing and is never without his sketchbook. He lives in Bedford, England.